Peter and the Blue Witch Baby

ROBERT D. SAN SOUCI

illustrated by

ALEXI NATCHEV

A DOUBLEDAY BOOK FOR YOUNG READERS

A Doubleday Book for Young Readers
Published by Random House Children's Books
a division of Random House, Inc.
1540 Broadway, New York, New York 10036

Visit us on the Web! www.randomhouse.com/kids
Educators and librarians, for a variety of teaching tools, visit us at
www.randomhouse.com/teachers

Library of Congress Cataloging-in-Publication Data
San Souci, Robert D.
   Peter and the blue Witch Baby / retold by Robert D. San Souci; illustrated by Alexi Natchev.
      p. cm.
   Summary: When the Tsar goes courting the Little Sister of the Sun, a jealous witch threatens
to destroy him and his kingdom.
   ISBN 0-385-32269-0
   [1. Fairy tales. 2. Folklore—Russia.] I. Natchev, Alexi, ill. II. Title.

PZ8.S248 Pe 2000
398.2'0947'02—dc21
[E]   99-088537

The text of this book is set in 18-point Caslon Antique.
Book design by Debora Smith
Manufactured in the United States of America
September 2000
10 9 8 7 6 5 4 3 2 1

Best wishes to my good friend and fellow writer, Patricia Kite,
whose good humor and support are treasures!
—R.S.S.

For my father
—A.N.

Long, long ago, there was a handsome young Tsar named Peter. He ruled wisely, and his kingdom prospered. But he was lonely and longed to marry. Many young women came to present themselves to Peter, but none captured his heart.

One day Molnya, a lovely, raven-haired woman, came to see the Tsar. Peter liked her wit and charm. But he was chilled by the hungry way she looked at him, like a snake creeping up on a bird. "Alas, fair lady," he said, "not you, but someone as yet unknown to me, will claim my heart."

At his words, Molnya let out a deafening screech. The astonished Tsar and his court watched as her eyes became huge and owlish. Her tongue, forked like a snake's, flickered over her black metal teeth. For she was a witch of the wickedest sort.

Pointing a crooked finger at the Tsar, she cried, "You will regret turning me away! When you find your hoped-for bride, your ruin will be at hand." Then she spun round and round so fast she became a dark, howling wind, and flew from the throne room.

For a time, the fearful Tsar gave up his search for a bride. But he forgot the witch's curse when he saw a painting of a golden-haired beauty. Instantly he knew she was the woman he wanted to marry. When he asked who she was, his chamberlain said, "That is the Little Sister of the Sun. She lives in a cloud castle to the east across the plains, beyond the forest, behind the mountains. It is a long and dangerous journey."

"Even so," said Peter stoutly, "I will go and ask her hand in marriage. And I will give her the three greatest marvels I own." These were a pebble, a seed, and a blue glass bead—and all of them were magic.

The morning Peter was to set out, an old woman came to the doors of the palace carrying a baby. "Be merciful, O Mighty Tsar," the woman pleaded. "Take this orphan into your household."

Peter's heart melted when he saw the pretty little girl. But when she smiled, her teeth were black as an iron cooking pot.

Peter turned to question the old woman, but she was gone. Eager to be on his way, the tender-hearted Tsar gave the baby into the care of his servants. Riding his finest horse, he set out to find the cloud castle of the Little Sister of the Sun.

Peter rode until he came to an immense, empty plain, where a giant sat forlornly.

Peter reined in his horse and asked, "How far is it to the cloud castle of the Little Sister of the Sun?"

"It is across the plains," the giant answered, sighing.

"Why are you so sad?" asked Peter.

"I am Water-Bringer," answered the giant. "My lifework is to dig the channels for rivers. But the springs that feed the rivers here have gone dry, so I must die."

Kindhearted Peter took the blue bead from his pouch. "I still have two gifts for the Little Sister of the Sun," he told himself. When he threw down the bead, a spring gushed forth. Water-Bringer roared his thanks, and at once began to dig the course for a new river.

Peter rode until he came to a vast forest. There he met a second sad-faced giant, sitting among the trees. All the leaves were brown and brittle.

"How far to the cloud castle of the Sun's Little Sister?" Peter asked.

"It is beyond the forest," answered the sorrowful giant.

"Why are you so unhappy?" asked Peter.

"I am Forest-Keeper," said the giant. "But my forest is dying, and I must die with it."

Peter knew that if he used the magic seed, he would have only one wonder to give to the Little Sister of the Sun. Still, he took it from his pouch and threw it down. Instantly there sprouted a new forest of towering, healthy trees.

"Thank you!" boomed Forest-Keeper. He began watering and caring for the trees as a gardener tends his flowers.

On and on Peter rode. At last he reached a chain of once-mighty mountains, now crumbling into dust. Towering above them was a third giant.

"How far am I from the cloud castle of the Little Sister of the Sun?" Peter asked.

"On the other side of the mountains, you will find only empty sky," said the giant. "There hangs the cloud castle."

Peter thanked him, then asked, "Why are you so sad?"

"I am Mountain-Stacker," answered the giant. "I pile up mountains to wall off the world from the emptiness beyond. But I have no more mountains to stack up. When they are gone to dust, I will die."

Though it pained him to use his last gift, Peter threw down his magic pebble. Then there arose range upon range of mountains. With a shout of thanks, Mountain-Stacker began rebuilding the walls of the earth.

Atop the mountain wall, Peter saw endless blue sky. Far off
floated the cloud castle. Below him a bridge of mist stretched to
the open gates. Though the bridge looked fragile, Peter spurred
on his horse and rode across it.

Waiting in the courtyard was the Little Sister of the Sun.
She was more beautiful than her painting, with hair like spun
gold and eyes as blue as mountain lakes.

Peter dropped to his knees. "I have come to ask your hand in marriage," he said. "But I no longer have the marvels I meant to give you."

"Your company is a gift," said the Sun's Little Sister, smiling. "I have few visitors in this lonely place. As for marriage—who can say? We must get to know each other first."

Then she showed him all the wonders of her castle. And it seemed to Peter, as they talked and laughed together, that she had taken a liking to him. He had never felt so happy.

They climbed to the topmost tower. There the Sun's Little Sister showed him a round window. "Through this," she said, "you can see any place in the world."

Anxious to know how things were at home, Peter asked to see his palace. He was shocked to see that it was in ruins: the roof was gone; the walls were broken and crumbling.

"I must return at once!" he cried.

Then the Little Sister of the Sun begged, "Be careful, dear Peter, for my heart goes with you."

Away Peter rode, along the bridge of mist, over the mountains, through the forest, across the plains. The giants he had helped called out greetings to him, but he did not pause.

When Peter reached his ruined palace, he heard a ringing sound—CLING! CLANG!—as though a great metal hammer were striking a huge anvil. Dismounting, he crept up to the wall and peeped through a hole. Inside sat a huge baby girl, her skin as blue as the sky, sucking her thumb.

Suddenly she pulled out her thumb and sniffed the air. Her mouth opened, and Peter saw rows of sharp black iron teeth. The baby snapped her teeth together—CLING! CLANG!

With a roar, she stood up, towering head and shoulders above the crumbling walls. She grabbed for Peter, but he scrambled through a tiny opening into a cupboard. He heard the Witch Baby's hands scrabbling at the wall that protected him.

Then a little gray mouse popped out of a crack in the wall. "Peter," said the mouse, "in the corner is a dulcimer. Play a lullaby on it."

Peter took the dusty instrument and began to play. The Witch Baby paused to listen. She put her thumb in her mouth; her eyes began to close.

"Keep playing," warned the mouse, "or she will wake up."

"What has happened?" asked Peter, playing all the while.

"That monster is the witch Molnya. You yourself brought her into the palace disguised as a little baby. She grew like a weed, and with her terrible teeth, she gobbled up everything."

"What am I to do?" Peter wondered. "I cannot play forever. I will never see the Sun's Little Sister again."

"I will play while you escape. Be quick," said the mouse.

Peter thanked the gray mouse and slipped away. Just as he swung into his saddle, the Witch Baby woke up. Oh, how she gnashed her teeth! CLING! CLANG! CLING! CLANG! She swelled up bigger and bigger, until she was half again as high as the palace. Then she jumped up and down so that the last walls of the palace fell to rubble around her, and she charged after Peter.

The Tsar heard a clamor—CLING! CLANG!—behind him. He looked back, and there was the huge Witch Baby. Her eyes flashed and her teeth rang—CLING! CLANG!—as she snapped her jaws. She ran with long strides, faster than Peter's horse could gallop. She would soon catch him, though Peter was carried faster than the wind across the plains.

But when she was so close that his ears were ringing with the sound of her teeth— CLING! CLANG!— Water-Bringer saw them. Quickly the giant changed the course of a river so that the flood ran between Peter and the Witch Baby. Instantly the water gathered into a deep, broad lake.

The Witch Baby had to swim, and it took her a long time to get across. Peter raced ahead, never looking back. His only thought was to reach the cloud castle of the Little Sister of the Sun.

All too soon, the Witch Baby splashed out of the lake and came thundering after Peter. Closer and closer she came, until she was right behind him. Peter could hear her snapping teeth—CLING! CLANG!—almost at his back. She would have caught him, but Peter was near the forest. Though it grieved him, Forest-Keeper pulled up armfuls of great oaks and hurled them in front of the Witch Baby. Then the monster had to gnaw through the pile with her iron teeth.

Peter's horse galloped ahead. But soon he heard the dreadful sound—CLING! CLANG!—right behind him. He turned and saw that the Witch Baby was almost upon him. CLING! CLANG! CLING! CLANG! went her teeth as she snapped at him. One bite took away a piece of his horse's tail. With the next bite she would finish Peter!

Luckily, Peter had reached the mountains. Grateful Mountain-Stacker tore up the biggest mountain he could find and flung it down in front of the Witch Baby. And another on top of that. Then she had to tear and chew her way through them, while Peter reached the edge of the world.

There he saw the cloud castle with its bridge of mist. The Little Sister of the Sun urged him, "Faster, dear Peter!"

The Witch Baby raged after him. Nearer she came—CLING! And nearer—CLANG!

Peter was racing across the bridge now. Behind him came the Witch Baby. CLING! CLANG! her teeth rang greedily.

Then three things happened at once.

Peter hurtled through the gates into the castle courtyard. The Sun's Little Sister called out, "Now, dear brother!" And the Sun, who had been hiding behind a cloud, blazed forth. He instantly dried up the bridge of mist. The Witch Baby, still gnashing her iron teeth—CLING! CLANG!—tumbled down and down. Soon the dreadful clanging became faint and then faded altogether into the bottomless blue sky.

Peter and the Little Sister of the Sun were soon married.
The little gray mouse played the dulcimer at their wedding.
With the help of the three giants, they rebuilt Peter's ruined
palace. Then the Tsar and Tsarina spent half their days at
Peter's court, ruling wisely, and half their days in the cloud
castle, where the sun shone brightly upon their happiness.